MYSTERIES & MARVELS
OF
OCEAN
LIFE

Rick Morris

Consultant Dr David Billet
Institute of Oceanographic Sciences

Designed by Anne Sharples
and Lesley Davey

Illustrated by Ian Jackson,
David Quinn, Chris Shields (Wilcock Riley)
and Nigel Frey

Cartoons by John Shackell

First published in 1983
by Usborne Publishing Ltd, 20 Garrick Street,
London WC2E 9BJ.
© 1983 by Usborne Publishing Ltd.

The name Usborne and the device 🎈 are Trade Marks
of Usborne Publishing Ltd.

Printed in Great Britain

Thornback
Ray

Bottlenose
Dolphin

Contents

Golden
Seahorse

Dragonfish

Boxfish

Cobalt Starfish

About this book

This book is a stimulating introduction to the marine world, with superb illustrations of over 100 species. The oceans cover about seven-tenths of the earth's surface and hold both the world's largest mammal, the Blue Whale, and the world's lightest fish, Schindleria, which weighs only 2 milligrams. Between these extremes there is a marvellous variety of fish, crabs, octopuses, starfish, corals, shellfish and sea mammals.

There are many mysteries of ocean life still to be explained and species new to science are being found every year. Worm-snails whose ancestors were alive 500 million years ago were re-discovered recently, as was a fish thought to be dead for 70 million years.

This book deliberately concentrates on the unusual, the extraordinary and the unexplained as a starting point to introduce readers to the fascination of the world of the oceans. It leads the reader towards an understanding of the interdependent web of ocean life and its species, many of which have survived over millions of years.

Pelagia jellyfish

Addis Butterflyfish

American Lobster

TRUE or FALSE?

Look out for these questions and try to guess if they are true or false. The answers are on p. 32.

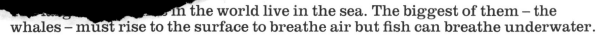

... in the world live in the sea. The biggest of them – the whales – must rise to the surface to breathe air but fish can breathe underwater.

The enormous Blue Whale ▶

The female Blue Whale is the largest animal alive today. She grows to over 30 metres long and weighs about 160 tonnes. This is about 25 times heavier than the world's largest land animal, the male African Elephant.

African Elephant

Blue Whale

The largest fish

Unlike whales, all fish are cold-blooded and breathe through gills. Most lay eggs rather than give birth to live young.

Whale Shark

Gills

Sharks are fish that have supple cartilage skeletons.

The Whale Shark, the largest fish, grows to over 18 metres long and weighs about 40 tonnes. It feeds on animal plankton. The baby shark hatches from a huge egg case – shaped like the mermaid's purse – which is laid by its mother.

All the whales are warm-blooded mammals. They give birth to live young and rear them on milk, in the same way as land mammals. Baby Blue Whales are almost 8 metres long when they are born. The Blue Whale, like many other large whales, eats nothing bigger than tiny shrimp-like animals called krill.

Great White Shark

The killer shark ▶

The Great White Shark is a fearsome hunter. It attacks and kills many swimmers every year. This shark is the largest meat-eating fish, growing to 7.9 metres with a weight of 3¼ tonnes.

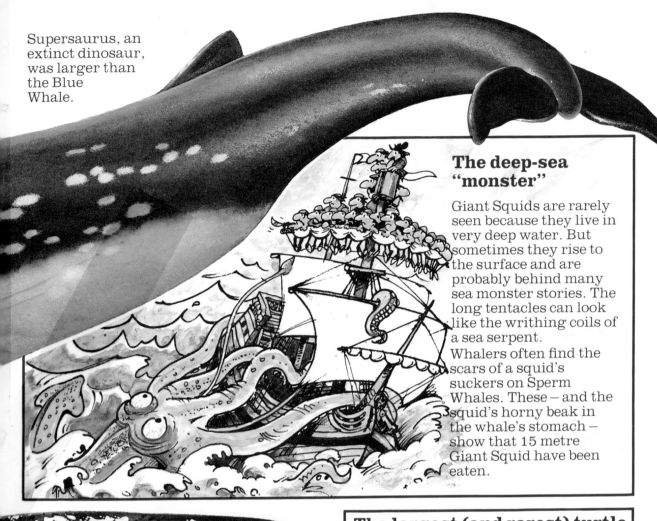

Supersaurus, an extinct dinosaur, was larger than the Blue Whale.

The deep-sea "monster"

Giant Squids are rarely seen because they live in very deep water. But sometimes they rise to the surface and are probably behind many sea monster stories. The long tentacles can look like the writhing coils of a sea serpent.

Whalers often find the scars of a squid's suckers on Sperm Whales. These — and the squid's horny beak in the whale's stomach — show that 15 metre Giant Squid have been eaten.

The largest (and rarest) turtle

Pacific Leatherback Turtle

The Pacific Leatherback Turtle is the largest reptile in the sea, growing to a length of 2.13 metres and a weight of 453 kilos. The female crawls ashore at night to lay her eggs in a deep hole which she digs in the sand.

TRUE or FALSE?

Big turtles cry.

The miniature sea world

The oceans are full of plankton – tiny plants and animals which drift in the sea. Most plankton is too small to be seen without a microscope, so the background to these pages shows magnified views. Each type of plankton has a distinct shape, often a startling geometric pattern. The young of sea slugs, crabs, starfish, barnacles and many fish start life as plankton, swimming in the surface waters and feeding on each other and the plentiful plant plankton. Ocean currents sweep them to new areas that the adults have not colonised.

Phytoplankton

The grass of the sea ▶

Microscopic ocean plants – phytoplankton – are known as "the grass of the sea" because they form a rich "pasture" on which animal plankton feed. Over 2 million million tonnes of new phytoplankton grows every year, mainly in Spring.

Krill – the food of whales

Krill is a large animal plankton – like a small shrimp – which eats phytoplankton. Many of the huge whales live only on krill, sieving it from the water. A Blue Whale – the largest whale – eats about 4 tonnes of these 6 centimetre shrimps every day.

Krill

Krill eat plant plankton and are then eaten themselves by sea birds, fish, squid, seals and whales.

A pile of baked beans weighing 4 tonnes (the weight of krill a whale eats in one day) would be 5.8 metres high.

The sea slugs and plankton on these pages are not drawn to scale.

Brilliant sea slugs ▶

Some of the most colourful ocean animals, the sea slugs, start life as animal plankton. There are over 3,000 species. Some adults, many of which feed on plankton, are small enough to crawl between grains of sand. Others grow to 1 kilo in weight. It is puzzling that some of the most colourful ones live in the depths where it is so dark their colours cannot be seen.

Most fish will not eat sea slugs. Their bright colours may be a warning that they taste nasty.

The Pyjama Sea Slug is found on the Great Barrier Reef off Australia.

Floating-garden Sea Slug

Mexican Dancer Sea Slug

Sea slugs have no gills but breathe through the tentacles on their back. The bright colours often come from their food – red from sponges and blue from jellyfish.

This sea slug stores green plant cells in its body. They absorb sunlight and produce sugar so the sea slug has no need to eat.

The Glaucus Sea Slug's tentacles help it float on the surface where it attacks Porpita jellyfish.

Glaucus Sea Slug

Plankton travellers

Some animal plankton travel long distances each day. Every evening, species which live deep in the water swim up to the surface. At dawn they travel back down again.

Some of these creatures are only 1-2mm long (a little larger than a pinhead). The journey of 400 metres each way is like a man swimming over 400 miles every day.

Sting-eaters ▶

Several types of sea slug feed on small planktonic jellyfish. The jellyfish's stinging cells kill most small creatures but the sea slug is unharmed. It actually eats the stinging cells which pass through the gut to the end of its tentacles where the sea slug uses them for its own defence.

Porpita's stinging cells

Porpita jellyfish

Collecting

Plankton also lives in fresh water. Why not take a jar to a nearby pond to find some? Look at the water drops under a microscope and you will see plankton darting around.

TRUE or FALSE?   Dynamite contains plankton skeletons.

7

Twilight and deep sea fish

The background to these pages shows how sunlight quickly fades away below the sea surface. The sea 300 – 1,000 metres below the surface is known as the twilight zone. The deep sea below this is totally dark and very cold. No plants live there.

Creatures in the twilight zone and deep sea have developed ingenious ways to survive and to find food.

The Coelacanth produces very few eggs but these hatch internally. Giving birth to live young has probably ensured the species' long survival. It lives at depths of 200-400 metres.

Coelacanth

The unusual stout pectoral fins are very mobile and may be used to manoeuvre over the rocky sea floor.

The peculiar double tail is a feature of primitive fish. Most species alive today, which have evolved more recently, have only a single tail.

Although the Coelacanth was new to scientists, it had long been known to fishermen in the Comoro Islands off Madagascar. They catch one or two every year. The 1938 Coelacanth was a stray. Since then specimens have been caught around the Comoros, 2,900 kilometres (1,800 miles) to the north. The fish's oily flesh is not good to eat but the islanders use the rough scales as sandpaper.

The axe blade shape of its silver body led to the fish's common name of Hatchet Fish.

The re-discovered fish ▲

In 1938, a fish which was thought to have died out 70 million years ago was suddenly re-discovered. Just before Christmas, a trawler brought an odd-looking blue fish into a South African port. Although it was five times longer than fossil specimens known to scientists, the 1.6 metre fish was identified as a Coelacanth. Over 80 have since been caught.

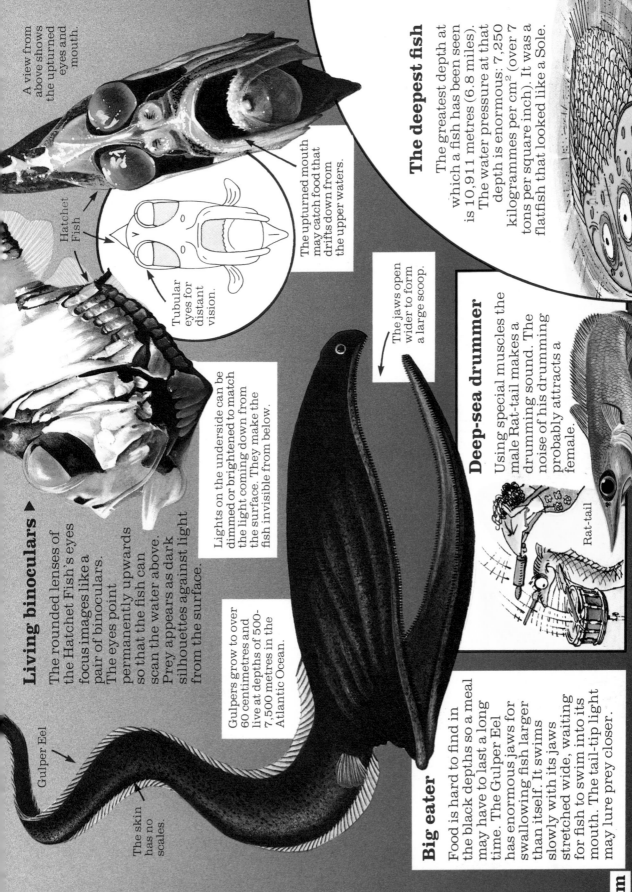

A view from above shows the upturned eyes and mouth.

Hatchet Fish

Tubular eyes for distant vision.

The upturned mouth may catch food that drifts down from the upper waters.

The deepest fish

The greatest depth at which a fish has been seen is 10,911 metres (6.8 miles). The water pressure at that depth is enormous: 7,250 kilogrammes per cm² (over 7 tons per square inch). It was a flatfish that looked like a Sole.

Living binoculars ▶

The rounded lenses of the Hatchet Fish's eyes focus images like a pair of binoculars. The eyes point permanently upwards so that the fish can scan the water above. Prey appears as dark silhouettes against light from the surface.

Gulper Eel

Lights on the underside can be dimmed or brightened to match the light coming down from the surface. They make the fish invisible from below.

Gulpers grow to over 60 centimetres and live at depths of 500-7,500 metres in the Atlantic Ocean.

The skin has no scales.

The jaws open wider to form a large scoop.

Deep-sea drummer

Using special muscles the male Rat-tail makes a drumming sound. The noise of his drumming probably attracts a female.

Rat-tail

Big eater

Food is hard to find in the black depths so a meal may have to last a long time. The Gulper Eel has enormous jaws for swallowing fish larger than itself. It swims slowly with its jaws stretched wide, waiting for fish to swim into its mouth. The tail-tip light may lure prey closer.

Deep sea

1,000 m

Lights and electricity

Many sea creatures can produce light. Some make their own luminous chemicals, others have colonies of light-producing bacteria living in them.

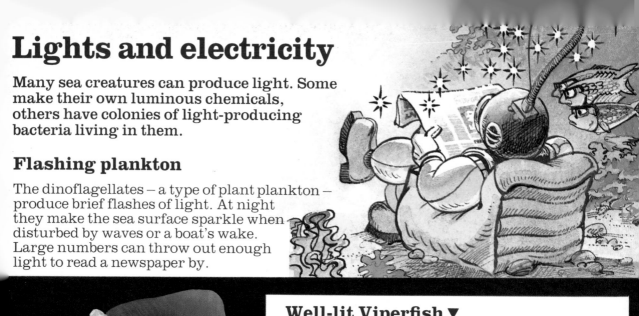

Flashing plankton

The dinoflagellates — a type of plant plankton — produce brief flashes of light. At night they make the sea surface sparkle when disturbed by waves or a boat's wake. Large numbers can throw out enough light to read a newspaper by.

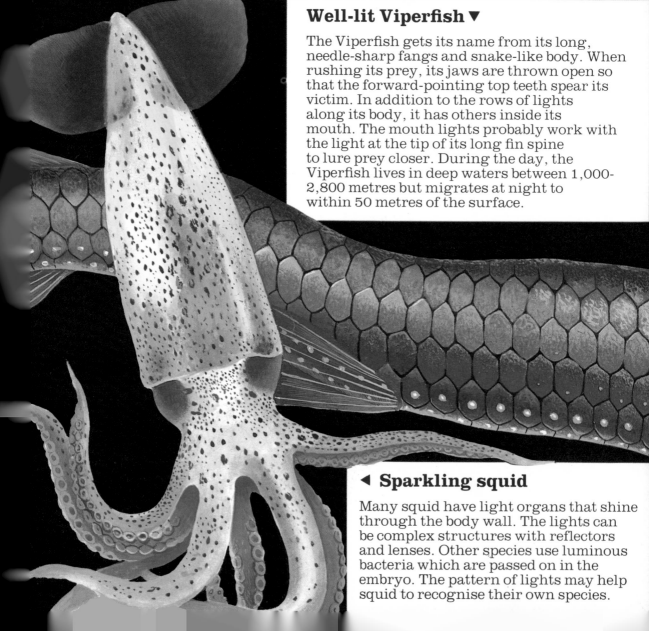

Well-lit Viperfish ▼

The Viperfish gets its name from its long, needle-sharp fangs and snake-like body. When rushing its prey, its jaws are thrown open so that the forward-pointing top teeth spear its victim. In addition to the rows of lights along its body, it has others inside its mouth. The mouth lights probably work with the light at the tip of its long fin spine to lure prey closer. During the day, the Viperfish lives in deep waters between 1,000-2,800 metres but migrates at night to within 50 metres of the surface.

◄ Sparkling squid

Many squid have light organs that shine through the body wall. The lights can be complex structures with reflectors and lenses. Other species use luminous bacteria which are passed on in the embryo. The pattern of lights may help squid to recognise their own species.

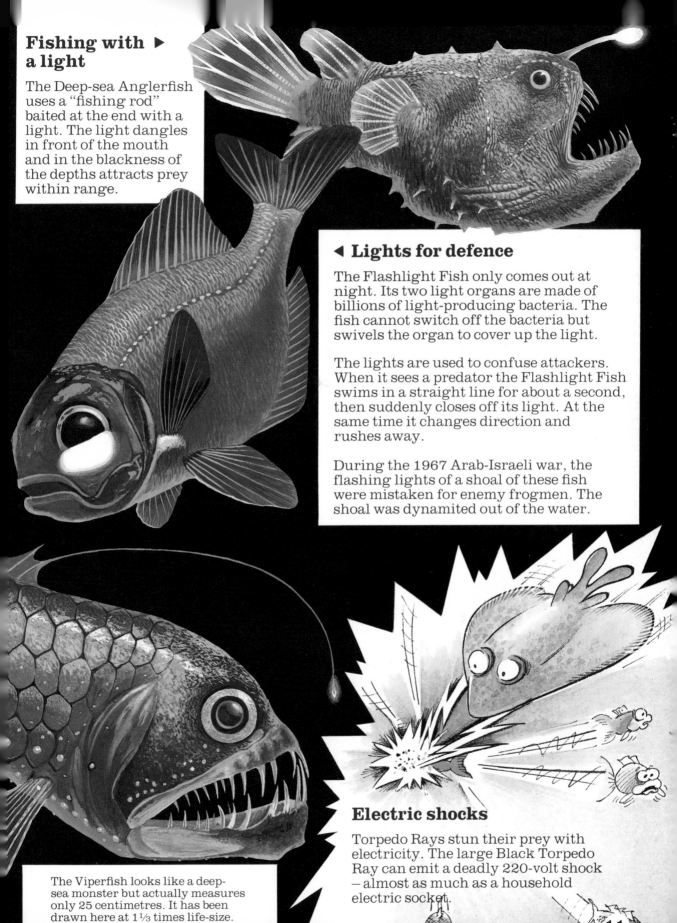

Fishing with ▶ a light

The Deep-sea Anglerfish uses a "fishing rod" baited at the end with a light. The light dangles in front of the mouth and in the blackness of the depths attracts prey within range.

◀ Lights for defence

The Flashlight Fish only comes out at night. Its two light organs are made of billions of light-producing bacteria. The fish cannot switch off the bacteria but swivels the organ to cover up the light.

The lights are used to confuse attackers. When it sees a predator the Flashlight Fish swims in a straight line for about a second, then suddenly closes off its light. At the same time it changes direction and rushes away.

During the 1967 Arab-Israeli war, the flashing lights of a shoal of these fish were mistaken for enemy frogmen. The shoal was dynamited out of the water.

Electric shocks

Torpedo Rays stun their prey with electricity. The large Black Torpedo Ray can emit a deadly 220-volt shock – almost as much as a household electric socket.

The Viperfish looks like a deep-sea monster but actually measures only 25 centimetres. It has been drawn here at 1⅓ times life-size.

Colourful characters

Sea creatures are amongst the most colourful animals in the world. The really brilliant species live in the sunlit surface waters of warm tropical seas.

Team colours ▼

In the busy waters around a coral reef each species of fish is decked out like a footballer in its own "team colours". This makes it instantly recognizable to other fish and to members of its own species.

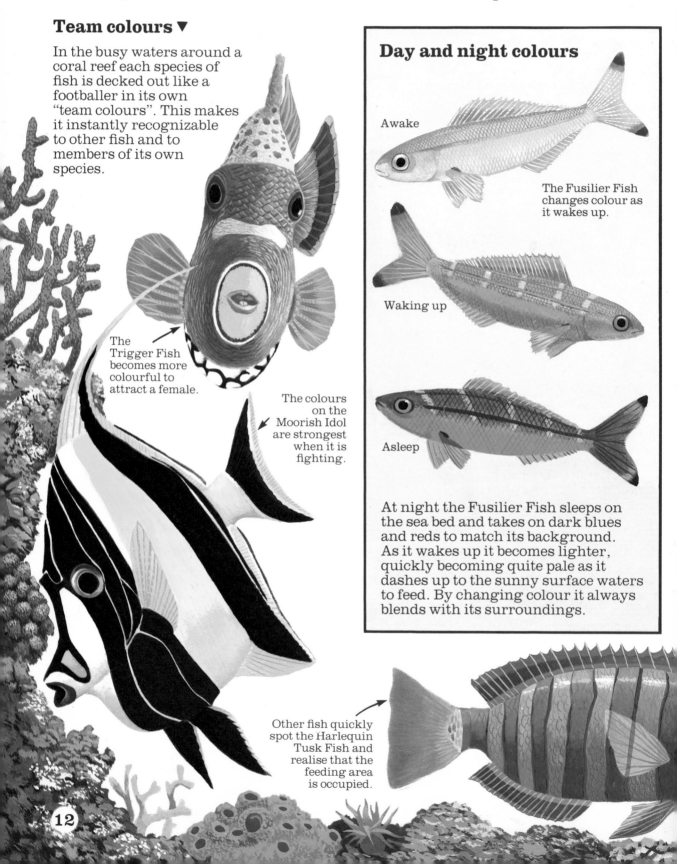

The Trigger Fish becomes more colourful to attract a female.

The colours on the Moorish Idol are strongest when it is fighting.

Day and night colours

Awake

The Fusilier Fish changes colour as it wakes up.

Waking up

Asleep

At night the Fusilier Fish sleeps on the sea bed and takes on dark blues and reds to match its background. As it wakes up it becomes lighter, quickly becoming quite pale as it dashes up to the sunny surface waters to feed. By changing colour it always blends with its surroundings.

Other fish quickly spot the Harlequin Tusk Fish and realise that the feeding area is occupied.

Warning colours ▼

Striking colours can be used to warn predators that an animal has a foul taste or is poisonous. The Sharp-nosed Puffer is extremely poisonous and other fish will not eat it.

In Japan people eat Puffer but it needs an expert chef to remove the poison and make the flesh safe. Known as *fugu* and regarded as a delicacy, the fish still kills people every year. In 1963, 82 people died of Puffer poisoning.

Puffers are protected by their warning colours.

Poison is found in the Puffer's liver, reproductive organs, intestine and muscles.

Camouflage colours ▼

Colours can be used for camouflage. Flatfish are the masters of this because they can change their colour and pattern to match almost any sea bed. They will alter their appearance in seconds when moving to a familiar sea bed. Unfamiliar backgrounds take them longer but tests have shown that they can even change to match a chessboard.

A Plaice takes on mottled colours to match a gravel sea bed. It will be overlooked by predators.

Multi-coloured mystery

Most starfish are slow-moving and live in the open. Dull colours would conceal them, so it is strange that they are brightly coloured.

Vermilion Biscuit Star

Rhinoceros Starfish

TRUE or FALSE?

An octopus turns white when scared.

Living together

Doctor's surgery ▶

Cleaner Fish run regular "surgeries" for larger fish who visit them to have pests and dead skin nibbled away. The Cleaners work inside the gills and mouth as well as over the bodies of their patients. Cleaners get a free meal for their work by eating the parasites. As the Cleaner swims it flips sideways, flutters its fins or performs unusual dances. These movements identify it as a Cleaner and stop larger fish from eating it. Cleaners can even work safely down the throat of a shark.

Grouper Fish

Grouper Fish

Cleaner Fish

Grouper Fish

Groupers live around coral reefs and come in various colours. They regularly queue up for the Cleaners' surgery.

Cleaner Fish are important to the health of the ocean's fishes. If all the Cleaners are removed from an area, other fish quickly move away.

At home with poison ▼

Sea anemones have poisonous tentacles that kill the small fish they eat. Strangely, the Clownfish is unaffected by the poison and lives among the tentacles, where it is safe from predators. In return, the Clownfish attracts other fish which dart after it and are caught by the anemone.

Clownfish

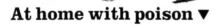

A special liquid seems to protect the Clownfish from the anemone's poison.

The waving tentacles of a large sea anemone.

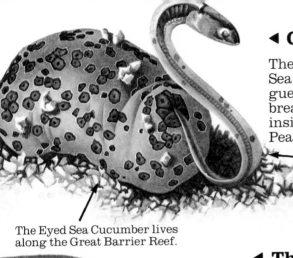

◄ Cucumber sandwich

The Pearlfish has a safe hideaway in the body of a Sea Cucumber. The Sea Cucumber tries to stop its guest getting in but eventually has to open its breathing hole. The Pearlfish then slips in, resting inside with just its head poking out. Sometimes the Pearlfish eats its host from the inside.

The Pearlfish wriggles tail first into its host. Young Pearlfish which stray into an oyster are sometimes found inside a pearl.

The Eyed Sea Cucumber lives along the Great Barrier Reef.

◄ The Moray Eel dentist

The Banded Coral Shrimp is another cleaner, with its own set of clients. The Moray Eel is one of its favourites. The shrimp works inside the Moray's mouth, picking leftover food from the needle-sharp teeth. Its nimble claws also pluck pests from the Moray's skin.

The head of a Moray Eel. Morays have snake-like bodies up to 3 metres long. They spend the day hidden in a rock cavity, coming out at night to feed.

The Banded Coral Shrimp waves its long white antennae to attract clients to its regular cleaning station in a rock or coral crevice. The shrimps often work in pairs. Although they are active during the day, they also clean sleeping fish at night.

▲ A real mystery

How do fish swimming in a shoal pass messages to each other? Is there a leader? How do they all manage to turn left at the same time? No one knows the answers to these questions. Communication between shoal fish is still one of the unsolved mysteries of the sea.

Garden Eels

◄ Garden of eels

An unusual fish lives in a colony. Garden Eels seem to grow out of the sea bed but they actually live, tail down, in holes in the sand. Their heads poke above the sea bed to catch food that drifts by.

Mimics

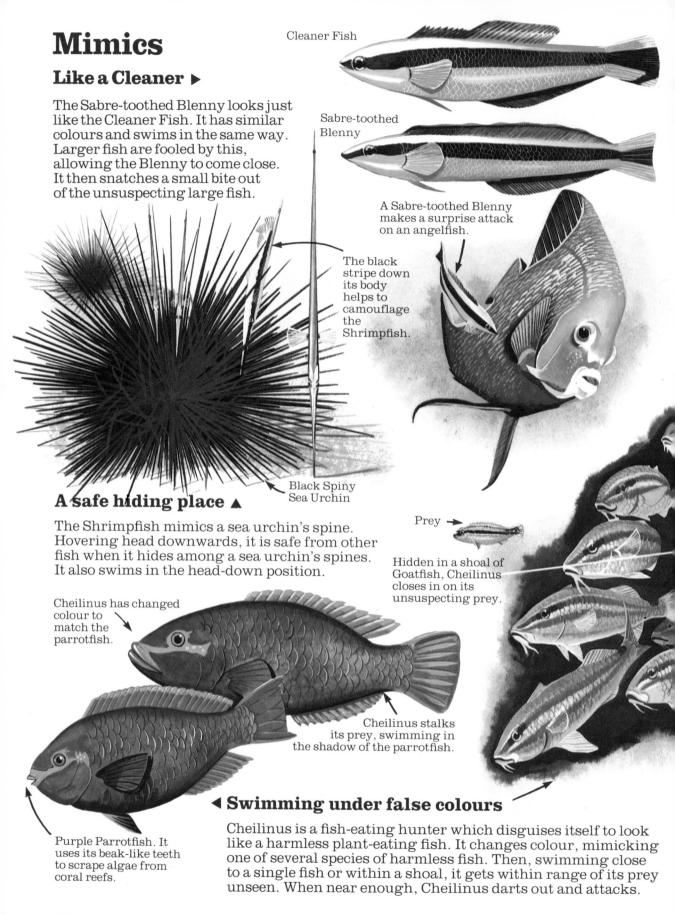

Cleaner Fish

Like a Cleaner ▶

The Sabre-toothed Blenny looks just like the Cleaner Fish. It has similar colours and swims in the same way. Larger fish are fooled by this, allowing the Blenny to come close. It then snatches a small bite out of the unsuspecting large fish.

Sabre-toothed Blenny

A Sabre-toothed Blenny makes a surprise attack on an angelfish.

The black stripe down its body helps to camouflage the Shrimpfish.

Black Spiny Sea Urchin

A safe hiding place ▲

The Shrimpfish mimics a sea urchin's spine. Hovering head downwards, it is safe from other fish when it hides among a sea urchin's spines. It also swims in the head-down position.

Prey ➤

Hidden in a shoal of Goatfish, Cheilinus closes in on its unsuspecting prey.

Cheilinus has changed colour to match the parrotfish.

Cheilinus stalks its prey, swimming in the shadow of the parrotfish.

◀ Swimming under false colours

Purple Parrotfish. It uses its beak-like teeth to scrape algae from coral reefs.

Cheilinus is a fish-eating hunter which disguises itself to look like a harmless plant-eating fish. It changes colour, mimicking one of several species of harmless fish. Then, swimming close to a single fish or within a shoal, it gets within range of its prey unseen. When near enough, Cheilinus darts out and attacks.

Small bags of yellow, orange, brown, red and black pigment are embedded in the skin. Muscles contract or expand the bags, combining them to produce a range of colours.

◀ Camouflage champion

The Cuttlefish mimics its background. Swimming over rocks covered with weeds and different coloured anemones it will change colour to match each background. Shoals of swimming Cuttlefish all change colour at the same time. Closely related to the squid and octopus, the Cuttlefish has eight arms and two longer tentacles.

Like squid and octopus, the Cuttlefish shoots out a cloud of "ink" to confuse predators. This ink is used to make the artist's brown paint known as sepia.

The cuttlebone, a Cuttlefish's internal shell, is often found washed up on beaches.

Matching the weed ▶

The Sargassum Fish mimics seaweed. Living in the Sargasso Sea, which is full of floating Sargassum Seaweed, the fish has clasping "fingers" on its front fins to pull itself through the thick weed. It is almost invisible to its prey, even having white body patches to match the casts of tubeworms on the weed.

Sea Dragon

The seaweed dragon ▲

The Sea Dragon imitates seaweed which grows off the Australian coast. A relative of the sea horse, it is covered with ragged flaps of skin that look like strands of seaweed. In common with other sea horses and pipefish, the male carries the female's eggs around until they hatch.

TRUE or FALSE?

The Pipefish mimics a pipe.

Marine hitchhikers

Hanging on ▶

The Remora is a hitchhiking scavenger, attaching itself by a sucker to larger fish. When its host finds food, the Remora lets go and feeds on the scraps. Remoras will also swim off in pursuit of shoals of passing fish. Hitchhiking is an easy way of travelling.

The vacuum sucker on top of the Remora's head is made from an adapted fin. It is designed so that the Remora cannot be detached from its host except by swimming forward. No matter how fast the host swims, the Remora cannot be shaken off.

Remoras grow to 90 centimetres, and up to a dozen may fix themselves to a large host, such as a Giant Manta Ray.

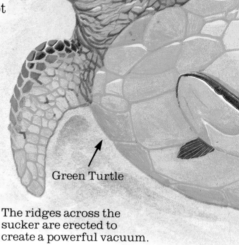

The oval sucker is positioned where the first dorsal fin would normally be.

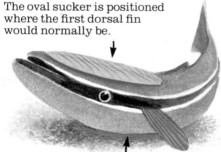

Remora

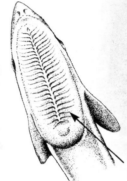

Green Turtle

The ridges across the sucker are erected to create a powerful vacuum.

Whale passengers ▼

Whales – particularly the Gray Whale – carry around thousands of passengers. Barnacles, no bigger than a coin, need a solid base on which to glue their shells. The large, firm surface of a whale is just as good as a rock or a ship's hull. Barnacles feed by sifting food from the water around them. The patterns they make on a whale's skin identify individual whales to whalers.

Acorn Barnacles are also found on rocks along the seashore.

Barnacles

Gray Whale

18

Islanders in the Caribbean and off north Australia use Remoras to catch turtles. When a turtle is seen on the surface, a fisherman ties a line around the tail of a Remora and puts it over the boat's side. The Remora heads straight to the turtle and clamps on. The islander then reels them both back in.

Outrigger canoe

The vacuum in the sucker becomes stronger as the Remora is pulled backwards by the line.

The Green Turtle often acts as a natural host to Remoras in the Caribbean.

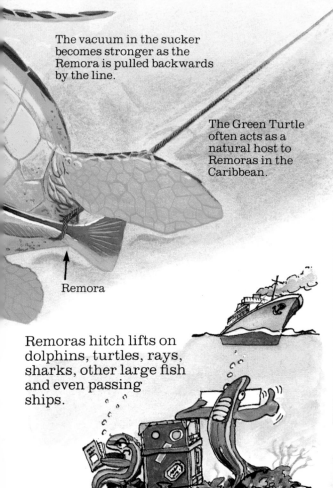

Remora

Remoras hitch lifts on dolphins, turtles, rays, sharks, other large fish and even passing ships.

A crabby lift

The hermit crab's passengers are sea anemones. The sea anemones travel around on the crab's shell feeding on the crab's leftovers. In return the crab is protected from enemies by the anenome's stinging tentacles. Large shells can have up to ten anemones on them, sometimes bigger than the shell itself.

Sea anemone

Hermit crab

Two male Anglers attached to a large female.

A male at the ready ▶

Finding a mate is difficult in the black depths of the sea. Some species of Deep-sea Angler get around the problem in an unusual way. When young males meet a female they attach themselves to her. Soon they become just another part of the growing female, living off her blood supply. When she lays her eggs the male is there, ready to fertilise them. The males spend the rest of their lives attached to the larger female.

TRUE or FALSE?

Crabs hitch lifts on dolphins.

Sea changes

Male

Female

The striking colour
difference between
sexes is unusual
in fishes.

Courting male

The male takes on different
colours when courting.

The Cuckoo Wrasse puzzle

PUZZLE: Cuckoo Wrasse are all
born females, no young males are
ever found, most old fish are
males and there are many more
females than males. How can this
be true?

The answer to this strange
puzzle is that Cuckoo Wrasse
change sex. Females do not
begin to breed until they are 6
years old and some become males
between the ages of 7 and 13.
This happens because the shoals
are dominated by large, old
males. When one dies, its place
is taken by a large female changing
sex to become a leading male. It took
scientists years to solve this puzzle.

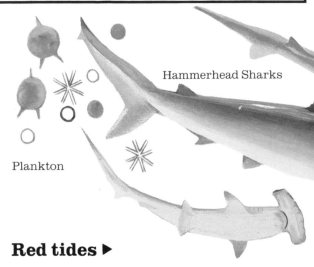

Hammerhead Sharks

Plankton

Changing tune

The haunting songs
of the Humpback
Whale have recently
been recorded and
studied by scientists.
They have found that
every whale's song is
different and that
each song changes
through the
breeding season.
Next season the
songs are
different again.
A single song
can continue
for thirty
minutes.

Red tides ▶

When some types of plant
plankton breed too rapidly they
produce poisons which turn the sea red.
These poisonous "red tides" kill everything.
The number of seabirds off South America
can drop from 30 million to 5 million
and a recent red tide off the Florida coast

Flattening out ▼

All flatfish start life as round fish. Young flatfish look like any other fish but after a few weeks their bodies begin to change shape. One eye slowly moves round the head and the fish swims to the sea bottom to lie on its blind side. Before long the round fish has become a flatfish. Its left and right side are now topside and underside.

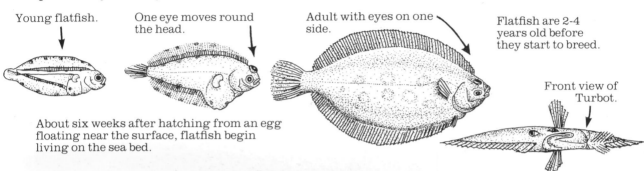

Young flatfish.

One eye moves round the head.

Adult with eyes on one side.

Flatfish are 2-4 years old before they start to breed.

Front view of Turbot.

About six weeks after hatching from an egg floating near the surface, flatfish begin living on the sea bed.

Plaice usually settle on their left side and Turbot settle on their right side. Reversed examples of each species are occasionally found. Flounders are less predictable, though two-thirds settle on their left side. Flatfish swim by undulating their bodies up and down.

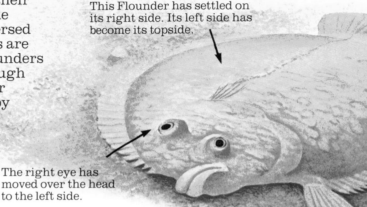

This Flounder has settled on its right side. Its left side has become its topside.

The right eye has moved over the head to the left side.

The pelvic fin was on the underside of the young "round" fish.

Manta Ray

Flying fish

killed about 100,000 tons of fish. As the usual sea life dies, strange invasions of thousands upon thousands of Hammerhead Sharks move in. They are followed by jumping Giant Manta Rays and schools of flying fish. Slowly the sea returns to normal and the invaders retreat.

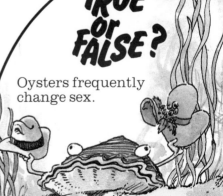

TRUE or FALSE?

Oysters frequently change sex.

The hunters' weapons

A Tiger Shark's teeth. The top two rows are in use. Those below are reserves.

Teeth ▼

A shark's teeth are its weapons for catching and killing prey. The teeth also tear off lumps of flesh to be swallowed. This style of feeding quickly loosens teeth. Nurse Sharks cope by moulting their teeth and growing a new set every 8 days. Other sharks have one set of teeth in action and 3 or 4 rows in reserve, ready to move forward and replace teeth as they fall out.

Tiger Shark ↑

◄ Tusks

The Walrus roots in the mud of the sea bed, hunting for shellfish. It locates them with its sensitive whiskers and digs them out with its long tusks.

Cunning hunter ▶

...when near enough, the bear dives and then surfaces at speed under the ice floe...

The Polar Bear is a skilled hunter. When the ice is breaking up in Spring, it needs great cunning to catch a seal. Spotting one on an ice floe, it swims towards the seal with only its nose above water and...

Sonar clicks

Dolphins "talk" a lot, using whistles to communicate with each other. Much higher frequency clicks are used when hunting, probably to locate their quarry. Recent research suggests the high-pitched sounds may also stun fish, so the dolphin can make an easy catch.

Bottlenose Dolphin

TRUE or FALSE?

The Geographic Cone harpoons people.

Strong suckers ▶

The suckers on a starfish's arms are extremely powerful. They can exert a steady pressure for a very long time. Using this strength, a starfish can open shellfish that have very strong muscles. Starfish dine on oysters, mussels and scallops.

The shells are prised open just a couple of millimetres, enough for the starfish to squeeze its stomach through the gap to digest the shellfish's flesh. Starfish always eat by wrapping their stomach around their prey.

A starfish preparing to open a mussel.

...battering the floe so hard the seal is thrown into the water. It is swiftly killed with one blow of the bear's powerful paw.

Defence and escape

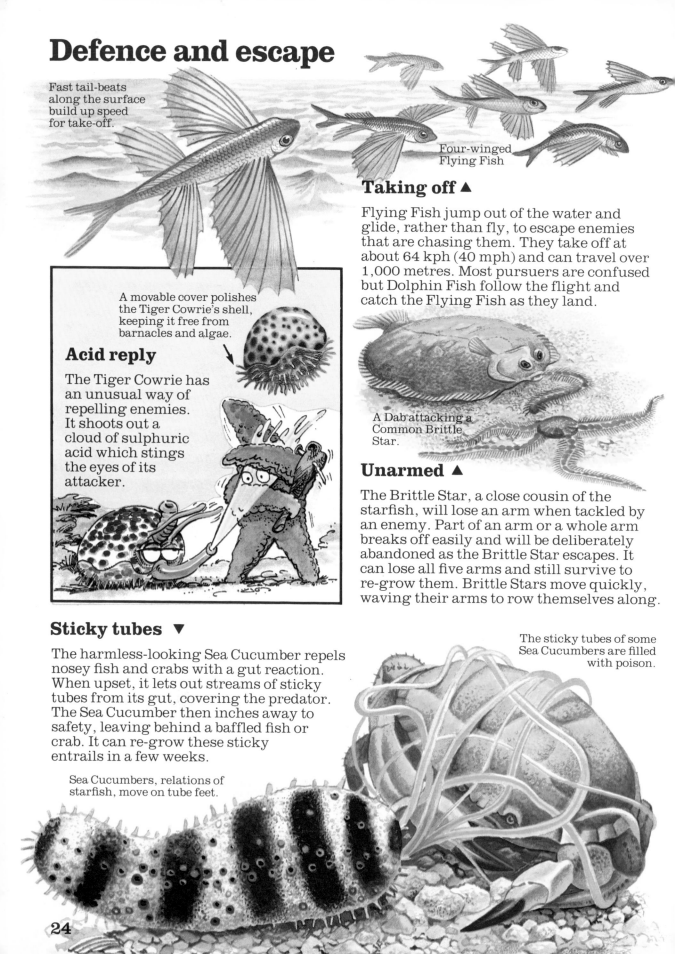

Fast tail-beats along the surface build up speed for take-off.

Four-winged Flying Fish

Taking off ▲

Flying Fish jump out of the water and glide, rather than fly, to escape enemies that are chasing them. They take off at about 64 kph (40 mph) and can travel over 1,000 metres. Most pursuers are confused but Dolphin Fish follow the flight and catch the Flying Fish as they land.

A movable cover polishes the Tiger Cowrie's shell, keeping it free from barnacles and algae.

Acid reply

The Tiger Cowrie has an unusual way of repelling enemies. It shoots out a cloud of sulphuric acid which stings the eyes of its attacker.

A Dab attacking a Common Brittle Star.

Unarmed ▲

The Brittle Star, a close cousin of the starfish, will lose an arm when tackled by an enemy. Part of an arm or a whole arm breaks off easily and will be deliberately abandoned as the Brittle Star escapes. It can lose all five arms and still survive to re-grow them. Brittle Stars move quickly, waving their arms to row themselves along.

Sticky tubes ▼

The harmless-looking Sea Cucumber repels nosey fish and crabs with a gut reaction. When upset, it lets out streams of sticky tubes from its gut, covering the predator. The Sea Cucumber then inches away to safety, leaving behind a baffled fish or crab. It can re-grow these sticky entrails in a few weeks.

Sea Cucumbers, relations of starfish, move on tube feet.

The sticky tubes of some Sea Cucumbers are filled with poison.

Blown out ▼

The Porcupine Fish looks quite small and ordinary until it is surprised by an attacker. Then it gulps in water, blowing itself up to football size. The spines on its body stick out all around like a porcupine. Most attackers are either scared off or unable to swallow the Porcupine Fish because it has grown so large.

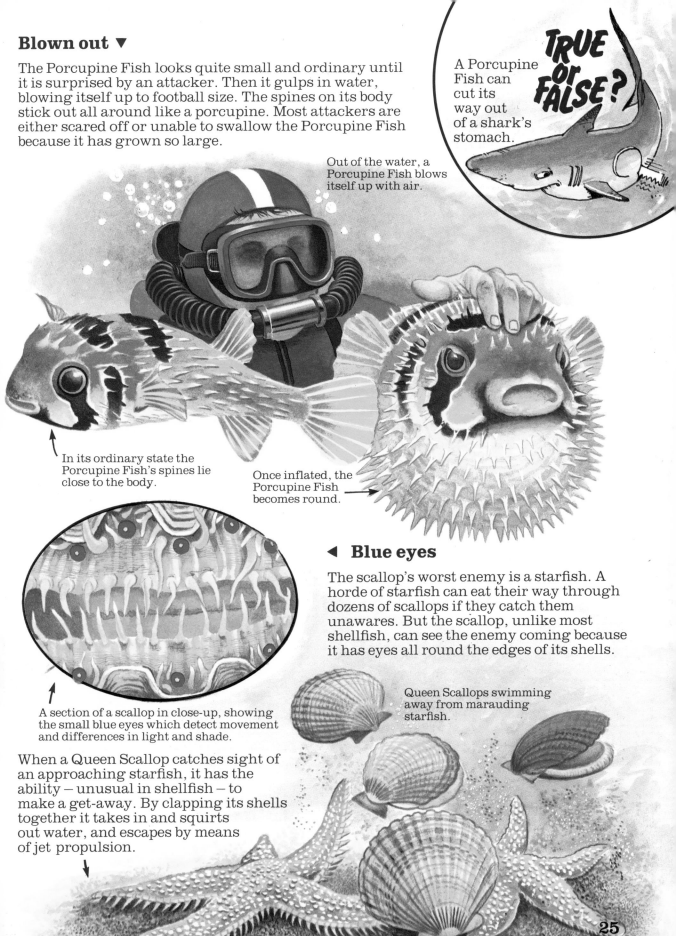

Out of the water, a Porcupine Fish blows itself up with air.

A Porcupine Fish can cut its way out of a shark's stomach.

TRUE or FALSE?

In its ordinary state the Porcupine Fish's spines lie close to the body.

Once inflated, the Porcupine Fish becomes round.

A section of a scallop in close-up, showing the small blue eyes which detect movement and differences in light and shade.

When a Queen Scallop catches sight of an approaching starfish, it has the ability – unusual in shellfish – to make a get-away. By clapping its shells together it takes in and squirts out water, and escapes by means of jet propulsion.

◄ Blue eyes

The scallop's worst enemy is a starfish. A horde of starfish can eat their way through dozens of scallops if they catch them unawares. But the scallop, unlike most shellfish, can see the enemy coming because it has eyes all round the edges of its shells.

Queen Scallops swimming away from marauding starfish.

25

Beware – poison!

The float is filled up by a gas gland.

Nomeid fish live among the tentacles.

Floating killer

Beneath its float, the Portuguese Man-of-war trails deadly stinging tentacles which paralyse and kill the fish on which it feeds. The tentacles – often over 15 metres long – are loaded with poison "harpoons" which, when touched, shoot into the victim.

The poison is extremely painful to human beings but, strangely, the Ocean Sunfish is unharmed by it, eating any Portuguese Man-of-war it comes across. Nomeid fish are also unaffected and can swim amongst the tentacles where they are safe from larger fish.

Ocean Sunfish feed on Portuguese Men-of-war.

Borrowed weapons ▶

The Mexican Dancer sea slug can feed on sea anemones without being harmed by the anemone's poison "harpoons". It actually swallows the minute spring-loaded harpoons without triggering them off. The harpoons travel through the sea slug to the tips of its orange "fingers". It is then armed with borrowed weapons which it shoots at anything that attacks it.

Anemone's stinging cell

discharged filament

trigger

barbs

lid

coiled filament

Blue-ringed Octopus

◀ Small but deadly

The Blue-ringed Octopus probably kills more people every year than any shark. The usual victims are bathers who pick up the octopus to look at it. Although the octopus's body is only 3 centimetres long it is one of the deadliest creatures in the world, producing poison more deadly than that of any land animal.

Poison fins

The elaborate Dragonfish carries poison in the spines of its fins. It swims along almost casually because its brilliant colouring is a clear warning to other reef fish that it is poisonous. If threatened, it will attack an enemy, jabbing at it with the poison-filled spines.

A Mexican Dancer eating a sea anemone.

Needles of death ▶

The most venomous fish is the ugly Stonefish. At the base of 16 needle-like spines are venom sacs. An unwary swimmer stepping on the Stonefish is injected with an extremely painful poison which gradually numbs the body and often proves fatal.

Stonefish are superbly camouflaged to blend in with the sea bed.

A Yellow-lipped Sea Krait attacking a Black-tailed Thrush Eel. Kraits grow to over 1 metre and may be found sunbathing on South Pacific islands.

Fangs ▶

The Yellow-lipped Sea Krait feeds mainly on eels which it detects by smell. It kills them with a series of poisonous bites along the body, injecting venom from its fangs. Unlike most sea snakes, the Krait comes ashore to hunt for birds' eggs and to lay its own eggs.

TRUE or FALSE?

The Swordfish's sword is tipped with poison arsenic.

Unusual events

◀ Stranded

Schools of over 200 whales have been found stranded by the tide on the shore. Why the whales run aground is still unknown. What is really baffling is that, after they have been towed out to deep water, they will often return to the shallows again. Scientists have suggested that the whales are diseased, that their sonar location system is confused by shelving beaches, or that the school has come to rescue a stranded whale. None of these theories really explain why whales should die in this way and it remains a mystery.

Pilot Whales are a species that often gets stranded.

Life-saving dolphins ▶

Sailors have seen dolphins rescue drowning swimmers by pushing them to the surface where they could breathe. This may seem like kindness but it is actually a natural instinct. A mother dolphin lifts a new-born dolphin to the air for its first breath and an injured dolphin will be held up at the surface by its companions. A human in distress sparks off this natural behaviour.

Bottlenose Dolphins are intelligent, social mammals which often co-operate with one another.

Apart from human hunters, the Walrus's only enemies are the Polar Bear and Killer Whale.

Death duel

An unusual battle between these two tusked animals was witnessed by a whaling crew. Each tried to spear the other in a deadly duel, the Walrus attacking with its 1-metre tusks and the Narwhal replying with its 2.4-metre horn. The fight was won by the Walrus which used its tusks to open up the dead Narwhal and feed on its blubber.

From nose to tail the Narwhal grows to 6 metres.

Sea anchors ▶

Families of Sea Otters swim and feed in the kelp beds (forests of seaweed) off the Californian coast. Rarely coming ashore, they sleep at sea. As night falls they twist and turn among the strands of kelp, wrapping it around their bodies. The kelp "anchors" keep the family together and stop them being swept away by fast-moving currents.

The otter's thick fur traps a warm layer of air.

◀ Bubble net

Fishing with a net of bubbles sounds an unlikely way to catch anything. Humpback Whales, though, have perfected a technique which works very well. Spotting a shoal of fish, a Humpback swims beneath it in a circle, releasing a stream of bubbles from its blowhole. The shoal is surrounded by a "net" of glistening bubbles and, although the fish could swim through them, they seem confused and remain inside. The Humpback then rises up to gulp down its captive prey.

▲ First one in...

The Adelie Penguin's chief enemy is the Leopard Seal which is large enough to swallow a penguin whole. Leopard Seals cruise around the ice-covered land where the Adelies breed. The penguins, wary of getting into the water, queue up on the ice, edging slowly closer to the water. Finally one dives in, or gets pushed, and if it survives the others quickly follow.

Adelies can leap considerable distances out of the sea on to land when fleeing from a pursuing Leopard Seal.

Leopard Seal

Only the male Narwhal has a horn. One of two upper teeth grows through his lip in an anti-clockwise spiral to form the horn.

Record breakers

Oldest fish

The Whale Shark is thought to live to 70 years or more. Halibut over 3 m long have been caught in the North Sea and are probably over 60 years old.

Largest shoal

The largest number of Herring in one shoal has been estimated at 3,000 million.

Longest migration

On their spawning migration from the Baltic to the Sargasso Sea, European Eels travel 7,500 km (4,660 miles).

Longest worm

One Bootlace Worm from the North Sea was recorded as 55 m in length (a lot longer than a Blue Whale).

Largest crab

The largest Giant Spider Crab, found off Japan, had a span, from claw tip to claw tip, of 3.69 m.

Most venomous

The Box Jellyfish's venom kills people in from 30 seconds to 15 minutes (exceptionally, 2 hours of excruciating pain). The poison of the Japanese Puffer Fish is 200,000 times more potent than curare, the deadly plant toxin used to tip poison arrows. Anyone unlucky enough to eat poisoned Puffer usually dies within 2 hours.

Most ferocious

Schools of Bluefin Tuna sometimes have "feeding frenzies", tearing into shoals of fish and cutting to pieces ten times as many fish as they can possibly eat.

Fastest fish

Incredibly, the Sailfish can cut through the water faster than a Cheetah can run. The Sailfish has been timed at 109 km/h (68.18 mph) whilst the Cheetah reaches 96-101 km/h (60-63 mph). Other sprinters are:

	km/h	mph
Wahoo	77.6	48.5
Marlin	92	57.6

Largest fish

The largest recorded Whale Shark was 18 m long, with an estimated weight of 43 tonnes.